Diary of a Psychopath

By

Steven Griffiths

For Karen and Peter Griffiths

For putting up with me still after all these years.

On June 15th 2013 the metropolitan police received a package containing the diary of Kevin Mason, the infamous Gallery Ripper who terrorized London between 2007 and 2009. This is the unabridged version of that diary.

12/05/2001

Right…I have no idea how to begin. I suppose "Hi diary" is a bit too informal for something like this. I guess I should just start writing, seeing as the only person who is ever going to read this is a psychologist that is really more self-obsessed than anyone I've ever met, yet he claims to have my best interests at heart.

Let me explain.

I'm fifteen, and having some "troubles". I've not been going to school and I've been going out drinking down the park, with my friends. Well I call them friends, they're more just people who I like to have around me while I do what I do, I can take them or leave them really. My Parents can't handle me, they try, but this is what it has come to. Having sessions with a middle aged man. Listening to him trying to relate to me, in order to help my "depression". This diary is his latest brain child. He believes writing down my feelings will help me to deal with them better.

The problem is, and don't get me wrong, it's a reasonable idea, but the problem is, I'm much smarter than he is. I know I am. It's obvious. I'm pretty sure I'm a genius of sorts, but I've never been tested. So I know exactly what he is trying to do with every suggestion he has. It's the same as with hypnotism. People who know how it works can't be hypnotised. So this, as an exercise, is pointless for me.

It doesn't matter though; I'll go through the motions. If it will make everyone else feel better. But it won't help me.

I can just imagine his old wrinkled face as he's reading this, hi doc, hope you're enjoying it. Don't know what you expected me to write here. Maybe I should scrap this and write what he'd like to see? Although that would be pointless in the scheme of things too. I may as well just play along. If he is one of my issues, then it's only fair that I put it down here. It's what he would want.

Anyway, I guess I've done my part. Diary written….I'm not sure how frequently he wants me to do this, so this may be the only one. How do I finish?

Bye Diary... no, that is a rubbish way to finish. Hasta luego. That works for me.

19/05/2001

Well, the doctor was not happy with my diary attempt. What a surprise. He's claiming I'm not taking it seriously enough. Not seriously enough? Can you believe that? I wrote over four hundred words! That's pretty serious in my book, considering I've avoided writing any sort of essay for as long as I can remember!

He says I need to focus more on my problems. He even said "if you think you're so smart, why are you seeing me and not sorting out your own problems?" I'll tell you why. I don't have a problem. I just want people to leave me alone and let me get on with it. But, as with most parents, mine want me to be a well-adjusted human being, it just doesn't always work out like that sometimes though.

In an effort to get me to "open up" as he calls it, he wants me to introduce myself and talk about me. He says starting from the beginning will give me a good idea of how I got where I am. It's a sound theory, but again, I know all this, so I doubt it will help. He also wants me to make sure I do this diary at least once a week. More if I feel like it...I doubt I will though.

In an effort to go through the motions set out for me, I'm Kevin Mason, currently fifteen years old, living in a small town on the border of Lincolnshire and Cambridgeshire. Fun? Right? Wrong, nothing interesting happens here. I think the most exciting thing that has gone on in recent history is a few guys a couple of years above me painted one of the porta cabins pink on their last day. Epic...Although it is still pink, so the prank itself did have some longevity.

That's me at the moment. I guess I have to talk about where I'm from and that. I wasn't born here. I've moved around quite a lot as a kid. We're not gypsies; my dad just moved a lot trying to find his perfect job. He never really did. But now he owns a pub in town, we live above it. And they wonder what makes a fifteen year old boy think it's okay to drink. I have a secret key to the bottle store. But I digress.

So, there is me, my parents and my slightly older sister, Gemma. She's okay. Definitely the favourite, but with me as the alternative it's hard not to agree with my parents for leaning that way. They'd never admit it, but we all know it's true.

I get on okay with my sister, I'm definitely smarter than her, but she always does better in tests and stuff. She studies really hard though, whereas I just assume I know the answers. Other than the arguments about who is smarter, we get on okay. She just leaves me to it.

That's about all there is to my history I think. Nothing exciting, fairly normal. I wasn't abused. If anything, they care too much, hence the overpaid psychologist who is giving me these menial tasks.

I can hear them all downstairs as I'm writing this. Laughing at one of those generic crappy TV shows that allow you to turn off your brain for half an hour at a time. I'd love to just burn down the studio that films those things with the presenters inside. Force them to make something of worth out of the ashes. But that's just me. I like a nice meaty crime thriller, where the killer or thief or something is always one step ahead of the police. They almost always get caught, which confuses me as they are clearly out smarting the police at every turn. Some people say it's because they wanted to get caught. Bollocks. It's because the good guy always has to win on TV. Otherwise stupid people get upset and worry about the dangers in their real life.

It seems I'm getting quite good at this diary thing, I've let myself ramble. I'm off to meet my friend, Simon. Some might say he's my best friend, and no doubt the doctor will make me write more about our friendship in the next instalment of my mental issues.

Hasta luego.

26/05/2001

He's a fucking dick!! Emotion! That's what he is claiming he wants! How I feel. I feel like he's a fucking arsehole! How's that for emotion. I would love nothing better to just leave this town behind and not look back...I could...I should.

I won't. That would devastate my family. That does not make me feel bad. If anything, I feel indifference to pretty much everything. I just don't want to make a mess. I would like my exit to be clean. And in order to do that, I need to play by their rules for a bit and finish school like a normal boy would.

Now before the doctor jumps on the fact I've just said I'm not normal, let me explain. I am normal, in the sense that all the right bits are in the right places. However, I am not like everyone else. If I was, why would I be in therapy? Everyone else doesn't do therapy. So I must not be normal. How does that make me feel? I bet anything he'd ask me that. It makes me feel indifferent. At a slight push I would say I'm mildly amused that I'm not like everyone else. I'm special.

Let me tell you about my friend, Simon. He is not special. Lived in this town all his life. Overweight. stupid....well not stupid, just stupid compared to me...average. Simon is an only child, so he thinks he is special. I blame the parents.

I would say he is probably my best friend. I spend the most time with him. But that is mainly because he will blindly follow whatever I do and not question me on my ideas. I don't like having to explain myself. You can see why I love therapy, right?

I've been told, now I've introduced myself, I should start writing down what I have done during my time between entries. I don't do much. This week, I went to therapy, went to school and listened blindly to people tell me about things I should know for my exams and then I went to hang out down the woods with my group of "friends". Not that exciting. It's a Saturday today, after I've finished my cigarette (I smoke, but not because I think it makes me cool) and finish writing this I will probably just go to Simon's house and listen to him tell me about his latest computer game. I'm not really into gaming, he always tries to get me to play. It's not my thing, and I have to admit, I'm not very good at it.

Later, I will probably go to the park again with a bottle of vodka stolen from the pub. The others will come, they always know I will bring some booze, so that's probably why they hang around with me. Or let me hang around with them, I'm not sure which way it goes.

Anyway, Hasta luego.

03/06/2001

Finally the doctor is happy with what I'm writing. He said I'm starting to really get to the root of what might be causing my problems. I have to avoid mentioning what he is trying to do, so this part is not going to be to his liking, but the next time I won't mention it. I just want to note that he's not complaining about what I'm writing now, which makes me feel...indifferent. But at least going through the motions is having some effect.

Not much has happened this week. The emphasis is on exams. I'll do okay. They're not hard, just laborious. Simon is panicking, I don't see the point at this late stage in the game, it's too late to learn it now if you don't know it already. Surely if you're going to panic about exams, you should do it at the start of the year, when there is a chance to change how little you've done in the previous years.

I don't have the panicking problem. Information tends to go in my head and stay there. Not all of it, but enough to get me through my GCSEs. Gemma is the same. She does revise though, because even though she knows most of it, she wants to make sure she knows everything. She wants that gleaming A on her record. She's just finishing up her A-levels. She'll do okay and be off to university after the summer. It'll be interesting to see how the parentals treat me once their favourite has flown the nest. I guess they'll just use her as an example of what to aim for in life. "You see what hard work and being good can get you, just look at Gemma at uni. That could be you". Wow, I cannot wait to hear that over and over again.

Not to worry, it is Saturday again and there is nothing to do this weekend. The week was pretty straight forward, no one was out as they were all revising, fools. I went to school, did some exams, and went through the motions. On a couple of nights I went to the park by myself. Got a little drunk, but mainly just watched the birds on the pond. I imagined being a hunter, hiding in the trees, slowly pulling the trigger, being God over the ducks, deciding which one lives and which one dies. That made me smile.

The rest of my day will be spent with a book on my lap so my parents don't bug me about revising and the importance of it again. But the TV will be on, and that's where my attention will really be focused. If asked, background noise helps me study and breaks up the monotony of revision. Textbook answer.

Hasta luego.

10/06/2001

Victory is mine. Two things. Number one, it's my birthday today, but I will get to that shortly. Number two, the old bastard is now happy with the way I am keeping my diary. He no longer requires to proof read what I've written. I don't trust him; he is a sneaky old crone, so I shall continue to write it, just in case this is some sort of trick. I am becoming accustomed to spending half an hour on a Saturday afternoon doing this though. I wouldn't say I'm enjoying it , but the habit is kicking in, so is the urge to have a cigarette whilst doing it. It seems I'm a massive creature of habit, maybe a little bit OCD. I'll give the doctor one small win here, this diary has helped me notice those things, but I am still indifferent to the fact that I am aware of it.

So, my birthday. What an event it is. I realise as I write this, that sarcasm does not come through in writing very well. Let's just say, when I was younger I used to get excited, then year after year I got more and more disappointed, with the gifts, (I'm not ungrateful, I just seem to have no use for what I get given), the party, the guests, every year was a bit of a letdown. So now, I don't get excited, I don't struggle to sleep the night before, yet go to bed really early in order for it to come faster. As with everything, I am indifferent. The same goes for Christmas by the way, not that I'm religious, my thoughts on religion can be saved for another day.

So, the plan for today is pretty simple. Fake a smile, be polite, say thank you. My mother has been planning a surprise party all week, I guess it's intended to pull me out of this "phunk" I'm in, as she calls it. The problem is, Simon let slip instantly about it, he can't keep a secret, so as soon as he found out, it was game over for the surprise. I don't mind that he let slip. In fact it's good, as I would only be angry if a party was thrust upon me unannounced. At least this way I can prepare my surprised face and attitude for the day.

I do realise that if for some unforeseen reason someone other than the doc manages to get their hands on this and finds it an interesting read, that to those people I may just sound like a spoiled, ungrateful prick. Let me explain to you, if you are reading this, I'm not like this on purpose. It's not my fault I feel indifferent towards most things, it just happened. It may be puberty, but I doubt it. I've tried to be happy, I've tried to feel anything. I do get angry, and that is the most common emotion I feel. Even the fact that I'm explaining this to an imaginary person who probably doesn't exist shows that I must care what people think on some level. The other side to that is, that if I found out that someone didn't like me (it has happened before, shocker) I still wouldn't care. Indifference is natural for me. I guess it's some sort of defence mechanism....I bet doc is smiling his stinking old face off somewhere because of this paragraph, I'm sure.

The doorbell just rang. That must be Simon coming to distract me as the party is being set up. I best go. Wish me luck.

Hasta luego.

16/06/2001

Something interesting happened today. Well two things I guess, but the second one hasn't affected me anywhere near the first.

So, the first thing. I was in the park late last night. I'd had a drink, but wasn't drunk. Just comfortably numb. I was just wandering around, not really heading anywhere, no real motive to my walking. The night was clear, so it was bright enough to see without a torch. Not much was going on in the park, there were some younger kids in the distance dancing about and making a lot of noise. I was walking away from them.

I got to a bench and sat down. I didn't notice it at first, but eventually, in the dim moonlight, I looked down, and there it was. Lifeless, eyes open and looking up at me. A dead squirrel. I nudged it with my foot, it was definitely dead. It didn't look like it had been killed, there was no blood. I think it just decided it had had enough of the mindless monotony and decided to pack it in.

Now I know what most people would think, a dead squirrel isn't the most profound thing in the world. But it wasn't the squirrel that affected me, it was what I did to it. As I was looking at it lying there, I felt the urge to see what it held inside. Like it was some sort of treasure being hidden from me.

I reached into my back pocket and pulled out a pen knife I had got for my birthday. The irony of actually getting something I have a use for this year. I picked up the squirrel in my left hand; it was light, and still quite warm. I felt a chill go down my spine and an explosion of excitement as I cut into its stomach. The blood and entrails spilled out over my hand as the small creature was emptied out. I must have sat there for at least ten minutes inspecting the creature, both inside and out. I was in a daze. And when I came back around to reality, I found myself smiling, a huge beaming smile. I was happy. More than that, I was ecstatic.

I'm smart enough to realise that this is not a good sign in terms of mental health. But damn, I've never felt like that before, and since, I think about other things like my family and friends, and feel nothing. I think about the squirrel in my hand, open, and I can't help but smile, and I have the urge to inspect another to see if it brings the same feelings up. I'm starting to believe I'm definitely not right in the head, but I also believe that I might not be able to be fixed.

My second bit of news. My indifferent, boring bit of news. The pub is not making any money, so my father is not renewing his lease and we are moving to a new town, a new pub....but hopefully not a new therapist. I wonder what the old bastard would think if I told him about the squirrel, I'd probably be referred. Maybe hunting is the thing I need to be happy. I wonder if I can take up hunting at the new place.

Hasta luego.

30/06/2001

Okay, so it's been two weeks since I've written anything. I could use the excuse that the move took up most of my time, but that would be a lie, what's the point in writing this if I'm going to lie to myself? The main reasons for not writing anything is, I couldn't be bothered, and without the fear of the doctor taking a look at my work, I felt no pressure to have to write something.

So the question is, why am I writing something now? Easy answer, boredom. That's not entirely true, it's partially right, but not the full reason. The real truth is, I was starting to miss it, and since the squirrel, I actually feel I need an outlet to explore how that makes me feel. I will humbly admit, on this occasion the doctor was right, probably not in the way he expected though.

I'm not worried about my reaction to what happened. I know it is a dangerous route to explore, but the way I feel normally, and the way I felt when I dug the knife into that dead squirrel's guts, I have to explore it. In fact, I've already started. I've been doing research. The more I read on the subject, the closer I come to the conclusion I may be a psychopath.

A psychopath is someone who is usually antisocial, intelligent, with a distinct lack of morality and empathy. On the surface they can seem normal and it's been proven to be very difficult, if not impossible to treat. I think I fit the bill. But I'm not sure how I should feel about this. I'm not sure I do feel anything about it. I obviously don't appear normal on the surface, otherwise I wouldn't have been sent to therapy. I wonder if the psychologist has "potential psychopath" written in his notes about me? Or he's just put it down to depression or teenage angst? It would be interesting to find out.

I've decided to go hunting. Not with a club, just by myself. I've read some books on tracking and catching animals. The thought of catching something excites me. That sounds weird, I don't mean sexually, it just fills me with emotion. It's the only thing that does. I should worry about these feelings, but I can't. I hope it lives up to my expectations.

Hasta luego.

02/07/2001

I did it. I went hunting. It was the most thrilling experience of my life so far. I've never experienced anything close to what I felt last night. Not even with the squirrel. Let me tell you what happened.

During the day, I went down to the woods, by myself. I took my knife, and a roll of thin, but strong wire. I had read a book on how to catch several different types of animal. I decided that for an inexperienced hunter like myself, I would try for rabbits. The theory being you set a type of noose outside a rabbit's warren, so when they come out through it, it tightens around a part of the rabbit's body, trapping it. So that's what I did.

It was hot as I was trekking through the local woods. I came across several rabbit holes on my journey, and decided to hedge my bets and set multiple traps all the way through the woods, taking a mental note of where I placed them. I felt like I was desperate to catch something, like my life depended on it.

After that I went home, and had dinner with my family. They said they'd noticed a difference in me and that I seemed content. I laughed inside, they had no idea what was making me so different, but if it gets them off my back then it can't be a bad thing can it?

After dinner was finished, I went up to my room. I didn't do anything. Just sat there, waiting for everyone else to go to bed, so I could sneak back out and see what I had caught. I remember I felt so nervous that I would find nothing in my traps. I so desperately wanted to catch something. I almost felt like praying for something in my traps, if I believed that there was a God. I was amused that the idea of what I was doing was almost enough for me to want to believe in organised religion, however I'm sure what I was doing would go against some of their teachings.

The sun went down, and my parents went to bed, followed closely by Gemma. I was already dressed ready to go by the time Gemma's door shut. I knew they wouldn't come in and say goodnight.

I slipped out of my room and headed downstairs through the empty pub. It was dark, and I did bump into things as I still don't know my way around this new place in the dark. But it wasn't loud enough to wake anyone upstairs. The door didn't make a noise as I slipped out, locking it behind me, and set off in the direction of the woods.

Before I knew it I was in a full blown run towards where I had set my first trap, getting there in what must have been some sort of record. When I did, I looked down at the first trap I had set. Nothing. My heart sank. Who'd have thought that this would give me such a range of emotion? I haven't felt like this since I was a child.

I carried on, not too disheartened, I had set many of the traps. As I continued though, I became more disappointed. Each trap I'd come to was empty. I started to believe I had set them wrong, and was close to tears that I wasn't going to realise what I'd hoped would happen.

As I approached the last trap, I heard frantic rustling. My heart almost skipped a beat as I looked down and there it was. A large grey hare, struggling against the wire, trying to get away from me as I approached. It could tell what was coming, and I felt so powerful as I reached down, grabbing it by the scruff of the neck, undoing the wire around it's leg and holding it up to look it in the eye.

It was full of fear. I could feel its little heart racing. I reached into my back pocket and pulled out my pen knife. I waited, savouring the moment as much as I could, but quickly I couldn't take anymore, and thrust the knife up into the hare's neck. I watched as the blood poured out of it, and as its eyes began to fade. The heart slowed and stopped. It was done. I had killed it. I was the master of life and death in that moment, and it felt fantastic. Nothing could touch me, I was king...no, I was God. I was the God I should have being praying to when I was waiting in my room.

I've never felt so powerful. Walking back, I kept looking down at the blood on my hands, trying to keep the feeling alive within me, but it was fading quickly. I got back to my room, laid on my bed and fell asleep happy for the first time, probably ever.

It has started something inside of me. I feel the urge to do it again...maybe with a larger animal, a trickier beast to catch. Even as I'm recalling this, the emotions are filling inside me, and the excitement of catching and killing again is burning.

I've got to go. My parents are making me attend a summer club to make new friends. I'll go along with it. Anything to keep them happy and leave me alone, so I can carry on with my own "hobby". I hope I haven't embellished this too much, but that's how excited I am now.

Hasta luego.

07/08/2001

I haven't written anything for a few weeks now. I should apologise, but I'm only going to be apologising to myself. So there is no point. I've been really busy and caught up doing my own thing. Life has taken an interesting turn for me I think.

I've never been more content. My parents are leaving me alone, I've been doing as they wanted and they seem to be happy with my attitude now. They call me proactive. It's all a show. The realisation that I can put on this fake exterior to keep them happy leaves me with ample opportunity to do what I actually am thinking of the entire time.

I've made a "healthy" friend as they call it. His name is Jim and he is complete nerd. If I'm honest, I don't really like him. He's opinionated, and smart, in a traditional way, but I can tolerate him, and that's what I need to do. It keeps my mum happy.

Since the hare, I have killed two more rabbits, three cats and a dog. I am finding the larger the prey, the more excitement I take away from the hunt. Two of the cats were strays, but the third, and the dog were pets. I don't feel bad that I've taken a pet away from someone. In fact, two days ago, I noticed a "missing" poster for the dog that I killed. I felt a surge of power, knowing that I had dispatched the dog, and no one knows it was me. I've taken to burying the bodies out in the woods and everything is done in the middle of the night so I can avoid getting caught. I'm getting very good at being deceptive. I'm almost certain no one even suspects what I get up to when the world is sleeping.

I've noticed something though. I do feel the strong urge to take credit for what I've done, especially after the dog and the poster. The satisfaction of knowing it was me who caused that poster to be put up was massive, and

I had to catch myself from telling Jim as we walked down the street and passed it.

He didn't even notice the poster; it's not the type of thing he thinks about, that pissed me off a little bit. I hope other people noticed it and thought "I wonder what happened".

Tonight I'm going to try to catch a fox. I'm not sure exactly how, but over the weeks I've been studying and increasing my tools. I've got a huge hunting knife now which I acquired from Jim's dad. It was just left out in the garage. I've also managed to get several lengths of rope and a set of boots.

I keep them all hidden away in a box, behind a false back I found in my cupboard, there is about an extra foot of space behind it. How apt that I would be given this room when we moved.

Anyway, the sun is going down, I best get ready.

Hasta luego.

08/08/2001

Things did not go to plan. I tracked a fox. There are lots in this area. It didn't see me as I sat in the bushes watching, waiting. I waited for about half an hour as it stood there relaxed eating something it found in the brush. I don't know what it was though. Eventually I decided it was time to make my move. I had my hunting knife in my hand ready.

I burst out of the bush and launched myself onto the back of the fox before it had a chance to react. As I jumped and grabbed it, the knife flew out of my hand and of into the darkness somewhere.

I had judged this massively wrong. My confidence was too high. The fox turned as I grabbed it and clamped down on my face, drawing blood instantly then ran off into the darkness. It left me with a horrible looking wound when I woke up this morning.

My parents instantly questioned me about it, I panicked and said I got into a fight. I got scolded by them, but I saved my own skin by saying it was a group of guys who were trying to mug me. That seemed to do the trick, but they insisted I called the police. I argued this, saying I had given as good as I got and am pretty sure I may have blinded one of them, so the police would cause problems for me and maybe push me back into a depressive state.

They've let it go now, after a lengthy protest. Although it was a failure, I still got a massive rush from the attempt. Having the creature be wild and fight back, even causing damage to me, it really got my blood pumping. I don't think small tame animals are going to do it for me anymore. The question is, what do I do now? I think more research and training will be required. I'll hold off until I'm ready.

Hasta luego.

16/08/2001

I've not killed anything for over a week now and last night, I had a major urge. One I had to fight pretty hard.

I've been keeping myself satiated by reading everything and anything about tracking and killing predators. The problem with predator hunting is, a lot of the text is tracking techniques and using a rifle to take down your prey. It lacks the personal touch I have had with the other animals I have dispatched.

So, my urge. This was interesting for me. Jim and I were at his house, playing a computer game. Well, he was playing and narrating how good he was at it, and I was dreaming about my next foray in the woods.

He woke me from my daze to get me to come with him to get a drink from the kitchen. As we reached the top of the stairs, the thought hit me. I could push him. I could push him down the stairs and he could break his neck and die, and I would be the one responsible for it. I'd get away with it too. People fall down the stairs all the time. I could really do it.

My hands were out stretched behind him and just before I made contact and gave him that shove to oblivion I stopped...What if he didn't die? He'd know I'd pushed him. He'd tell everyone that I'd done it. I'd be back in therapy so quickly, my private time would be taken away from me, and I would not be able to pursue my interests without being found out.

I pulled my hands back. I did smile though. I had the power in that situation. I could have pushed him, and he could have died. I chose not to. But I could have...

Hasta luego.

03/09/2001

Something has happened. I've not been able to kill since my last entry. I was researching still, but my time alone has become limited.

A week ago, I was woken up in the middle of the night. Dazed and confused I was told to get dressed and bundled into a taxi with my sister. I had no idea where it was heading, until we arrived at the hospital.

The foyer of the hospital was empty. Apart from my mother, sat on a bench in the entrance. She beckoned us over, her eyes were red and I think at the time I knew exactly what was coming. Gemma didn't.

She sat us down, and while fighting back the tears, she explained that there had been a break in at the pub when everyone was asleep. Dad woke up and went to investigate. He was attacked, and stabbed by the intruder. They rushed him to hospital, but he didn't make it.

Gemma instantly burst into tears and was embraced by our mum. I sat there. Numb. I wasn't sure what I was feeling. I couldn't help but go back to the thought that surely if the noise had woken dad up, why had it not woken me?

I realised I wasn't doing anything but thinking about that, I wasn't feeling anything either. No sadness, no anger, nothing. I had to do something. I faked it. I clutched my head in my hands and shuddered, hoping that rubbing my eyes enough would make them red and bring forth tears.

Since that night, we've not had any time to ourselves. Gemma and I have been smothered with condolences and affection, not wanted by me, at all hours of the day and night.

We've just returned from the funeral. I didn't cry. I didn't even try to fake it. I just sat there, staring into space as a box with a corpse in it disappeared behind a red curtain. Some people said some nice things about my father, but I wasn't really paying attention. I sat there thinking about what it would feel like to put someone there myself.

The wake was also a quiet affair. I sat in the corner nursing a beer I was allowed to have one, due to the occasion. People kept bothering me and stealing me away from my sinister thoughts. The thoughts that keep me happy. I smiled politely and thanked them for their kind words.

I've snuck away now to write this in private, but already I have been interrupted twice. It's frustrating when you're trying to get your thoughts together. I'll have to rejoin the "festivities" shortly.

I don't think I'll be able to write anything for a while; we have to leave the pub and move to a smaller house. My mum cannot run it by herself, and the lease was in my father's name. Hopefully I'll be able to put pen to paper at some point soon. But I can't say when.

Hasta luego.

09/09/2006

Astonishing. I had almost forgotten about this little diary of the macabre I had kept when I was younger. How strange it is to look back five years at the very thing that has led me to this point. How apt that it is this diary that has allowed me to take the final leap that was always going to be inevitable.

Let me catch you up.

After my father had died, my mother, me and my older sister Gemma moved back to a small house in Lincolnshire. It was in the centre of a small town called Bourne and there wasn't much opportunity for me to follow my passion. I began to get withdrawals, if you can believe that. This diary got packed away with my things and was no doubt consigned to a box in the loft. Potentially lost forever. If I'm honest, I didn't even look for it.

After that summer, my sister moved out to go to university, and my mother got a job. It's at this point I was able to create enough time to satisfy my urges. Nothing big, just enough to keep the blood pumping. Cats, dogs...a parrot. All pets. in the next couple of years I had racked up quite a list of animals I had seen off, and I was becoming better at covering my tracks. No one even suspected me. I had a good group of friends and was hiding my lack of emotion with great prowess.

I passed all my exams and got into university to study business. Not much happened in those three years. I still managed to keep my hobby alive, but being surrounded by other students and the pressure to go out and be social dropped my numbers to about one kill every three or four months.

I graduated, and that brings me to where I am now. Adding an entry to a diary that was lost years ago. Now I start though, I feel it is necessary to continue, not for therapy, but for documentation of my exploits. Especially now things have taken a turn. Let me tell you, I am shaking while I write this. The excitement is too much and my blood is boiling in my veins.

I've killed a person. A human. A friend. And it feels amazing.

I'm twenty one now, after university I walked straight into a job for a large firm in London. Low down, but good pay. I won't bore you with the details, it's not interesting in the least. For the move to London, I needed a flat, and as it turns out, so did Jim, the boy I made friends with before my dad died. We kept in touch and finally, a few months back moved in to a small two bedroom flat together.

This was a mistake he didn't know he was making. This morning, a box arrived for me, from my mother. I was at work, but Jim was home. When I got in, I found him sat with the box open and stuff taken out. This wasn't a problem. It was only old stuff from the house that my mother needed to clear out.

The problem was what was in his hand. My notebook. This diary. He was reading it. He looked up at me from the pages with confusion and fear at what he'd just read. He'd seen into the truth of who I really was. What I'd worked so hard to keep hidden from the world. I remember his mouth quivered as he uttered the words "You're a psycho". I saw red. I couldn't control myself. I launched myself at him, grabbing a bottle of whisky that was on the side and hit him across the head with it. The bottle didn't smash, but he went down hard. Before I knew it I was on top of him, continuing to hit. The bottle finally smashed and my hitting turned to stabbing. I must have stabbed him over fifty times. Blood was everywhere, and Jim was dead.

I sat there for about five minutes. In silence. Letting the gravity of the situation sink in. Instead of despair at what I had done, it was power I felt. This man was dead. Gone. Not coming back...and no one knew.

His body is on the floor as still while I am writing this. I'll have to deal with that. I'll figure something out. One thing is for certain though. I must not get caught. This is only the beginning.

Looking back I see I ended my entries with Hasta luego. How cool, even through the indifference, I must have thought I was using that. I don't think that will continue in my future entries.

10/09/2006

I've disposed of Jim's body, and I must say I'm pretty proud of myself for my quick thinking and ingenuity.

First, I moved him to the bath tub to contain what blood was left in him. Then I got to work clearing up the mess I had created in the living room. It is all laminate wood effect flooring so because I was quick enough there was no staining. There was a hell of a lot of mess though. I will definitely have to think of a better way to do this next time.

With all the glass and blood cleared, I had to deal with the body. I knew there was no way I'd be able to get him out of the flat in one piece without being noticed. I had to dismantle him. With a hack saw , I began to break him down and stored the pieces I pulled off in bin bags I had prepared. As I did this, I thought about other killers that ate parts of their victims. I looked down at the remnants of Jim and did wonder how anyone could find that appetising. Safe to say I'm not a cannibal.

With Jim loaded into five separate bin bags, I lined the boot of my car and loaded him in. I know what people think, a car in London, I must be crazy.

I did all this during the day. I figured it was easier to avoid suspicion. Hiding in plain sight. I was nervous, but that just extended my excitement from the act that I had committed.

Traffic was terrible. I drove out of London and after an hour or so traversing the roads, I was on the A1 heading north. I got quite far and pulled off onto back country roads. The roads were lined with woods, about every thirty miles, when I thought the coast was clear, I would pull over and venture for about fifteen minutes into the undergrowth with one of the bags and a shovel. I'd bury the bag, as deep as time would allow and continue on to the next spot.

I was rushing. I wanted to get back in time for when Jim would usually finish work. When I did, I waited until about 20:00. Then I called Jim's mum. Asking if she'd heard from him, because he hasn't come back and I can't get hold of him. This I think was my genius move.

Tomorrow, I won't have seen Jim either, and then the next day I'll phone the police and tell them I think he may be missing. No doubt I'll have to give a statement, but I've taken a sick day today, I'm pretty sure nobody saw me loading the car and there is no CCTV in this area. So as far as anyone is concerned, I'm in bed, ill. I even phoned my mum telling her I wasn't feeling well, and thanked her for the parcel she sent. I really meant the thank you too. This diary has awakened me to the person I should have been all along.

Maybe I should call his work in the morning to inquire as to whether he is there. That seems like a good move. I'll decide in the morning. It has been a long and thrilling day.

12/09/2006

It seems to have worked. The police have been over and spoke to me, and my neighbours. Jim is officially classed as missing. No suspicion is pointing in my direction. I even dropped the hint that he clearly wasn't happy living in London, although it seemed odd that he would move away and didn't take his stuff. His mother is very worried. I spoke to her on the phone, and reassured her he will probably turn up at some point soon. I couldn't help but smirk at this as I said it to her.

With the thought that Jim (or his body) will never be found, I am ready for my next kill. I may leave it a week or so until I act upon this, but I'm ready. Although I have the flat to myself, I don't think it would be wise to utilise this new found privacy just yet. As the hunt for missing Jim continues, I'm guessing there will be people snooping around and looking through his things. I will do a sweep of the flat and his stuff to make sure that there is nothing that will point to his murder. I'm even going to invest in a black light so I can get rid of any infra red evidence that may be there, I'm sure there will be.

The next kill will be prepared, not heat of the moment. Even sitting here with a cigarette and whisky thinking about it is sending me wild. I will pick a victim, someone who won't be missed too much. I will research their movements and pick a spot perfect for the act, and then I will dispose of the body. Possibly by fire. I can't afford to be travelling up and down the country digging graves for bin bags.

I've enrolled in a mixed martial arts class. I figure if I am going to pursue this properly, I need to increase my fitness and be able to defend myself if things do not go to plan. The first class is tomorrow. I best get some rest.

20/09/2006

I've found my victim. Technically my second victim, but in the scheme of the way things are going, officially I would say this will be my first in what will be a long list of people who will become my prey.

I should note. I am not killing these people due to a hatred of any sort. I am not discriminating between gender, colour, race or creed. I am killing to satisfy my own urges. The thing deep down inside me that is telling me to do this and fills me with so much excitement I could burst. Anyone will do. The selection is however based on how, when and where is best to carry out this act.

The first is a woman. A prostitute to be more accurate. I've been, for lack of a better word, stalking her for the last two nights and have come to these conclusions: She lives alone, and does not have any friends or family who visit her. Not that I've seen anyway. She usually starts her work at around eight in the evening down a dark side street about three miles from my flat. She seems to work alone and doesn't have a manager of sorts directing her money or movements, and it seems that she will either join her patrons in their vehicle or go with them to a hotel room.

My plan is to approach her as a client with my car and drive out to somewhere secluded. Once there, I will get her out of the car and do the deed. Somewhere mess doesn't matter. I've seen a few abandoned houses around the area. Maybe one of them. Once done, I shall set fire to the house and walk away knowing that nobody will be able to trace it back to me. I have a sticker to place over my number plate with a false number (but same car) registered to someone up in Scotland. If someone spots that, it won't come back to me.

I am thinking this plan is pretty fool proof, but I don't want to get ahead of myself, I will go over everything twice and ensure I am covered. My god,

I've not felt this good. Not with any of the other things I've done. I want to tell someone. I want to let people know I hold this kind of power. I suppose that is what this diary is really for now. In years to come, when I am finally rotting away in the ground, maybe someone will find this under my floorboards and the world will know what I have done. That though makes me content.

It will happen the day after tomorrow. I cannot wait.

22/09/2006

I've done it. The plan changed as the night went on. In a way I wasn't expecting it to, but I'm confident I'm moving in the right direction.

I went to the location where she worked. She wasn't there, must have been on a job already, so I pulled up at the side of the street and waited. Other girls approached me, but I sent them away, it wasn't them I was interested in. I had my sights set, and my plan made.

After about an hour, my patience was wavering slightly. But then she appeared back on the street, to her usual spot. I started the car and rolled up towards her slowly, winding down the window. As I stopped next to her she leaned on the door and said, with not much enthusiasm "hey handsome, are you looking for some company tonight?". I had to chuckle slightly at the cliché, but then I smiled at her warmly and told her to hop in.

When she was in the car, she told me her name was Sugar, but I knew it was really Sarah from my planning. I let it slide, and she continued to suggest a small hotel nearby that she often goes to, saying the manager doesn't mind if we slipped him an extra twenty pounds. I told her I had somewhere more discreet and adventurous in mind. She didn't seem to care, as long as she got her money.

I directed her to the glove box, where I had two hundred and fifty pounds in an envelope for her. She took it and put it in her purse. I wasn't worried; I'd be getting it back soon enough. All part of the deception, to get her where I wanted her.

We pulled up to an old abandoned factory I had found. The fence was broken and the door wasn't chained. There was graffiti everywhere, but no one seemed to have been there for quite a while, and there were no houses or cameras nearby. Perfect for what I needed. We got out of the car and headed inside. She seemed to get nervous, but the money I assume is why she followed me in. She asked me why I was taking her there. I told her it was adventurous for me and I'd set up a candle lit area inside for us.

When we were inside, I made her walk ahead of me, and as I followed, I retrieved my old hunting knife from the back of my trousers. It felt so good in my hands, knowing that it was going to be used on the ultimate prey.

We got to the end of the corridor which opens up into what must have been the factory warehouse floor when it was functioning. She looked in, and not being able to see the area I told her about, turned and asked "where is it baby?" The knife was behind my back, and I pointed with my other hand saying it was at the other end of the room in a small office that was there. As she looked across the factory floor, I thrust the knife out with all my strength, plunging it into her back. She yelped with pain and dropped to her knees. I pulled on her hair exposing her throat and ran the freshly sharpened knife across her neck, opening it with a spray of blood. She gasped and choked for a bit trying to crawl away from me as she clutched her wound. I stepped over her and squatted down to look her in the eyes. She scrambled with one last effort to grab me, I hopped back slightly letting her drop to the floor and smiled as the light finally extinguished from her eyes with a last gargled breath.

I sat there looking at her for a while, contemplating the difference I felt between this and what happened with Jim. I was so much more proud of this. I thought about how I would set fire to the factory and let her burn inside, only to be discovered afterwards by the firemen. No, that's not what I wanted. She needed to be displayed. I did this, and people needed to see my work.

I propped up her body against a set of wooden staging that was left along with the building. I tied her arms out open, above her head and sliced open her belly. From her purse I took the envelope of money and began stuffing it into the open gash in her stomach. I then took her makeup and proceeded to paint her face with so much of it she almost looked like a clown.

I'm not sure why I displayed her in this manner. I definitely was not thinking of the statement it could have been making, that this was the price of her womanhood, but that is apt. I just wanted someone to see it and appreciate what I'd done.

Before I left, I spent about an hour searching the entire area to ensure there was no evidence of me having been there, after which, I took one final look at my work and promptly left. I got in my car and drove straight home, with music blaring and me smashing my hand on my steering wheel to the beat. I've never felt more alive. Once home, I put my clothes in a bin bag to be burned later, and had a shower. That brings me to now. Now I sit here writing and wondering how long it will be until someone finds her? How long will it be until my next kill? How will I display that one? Who will it be? Will I ever be caught? The answer to this final question I am already certain of. No. I will not be caught. I'll not go down in an epic hail of gunfire like in the movies. I will quietly continue my work in the shadows of society, leaving them to wonder when I will strike next, and why the police are unable to stop me. It will only stop, when I am satisfied, and I'm not sure I ever will be.

27/09/2006

Five days! It took five days for my work to be found. I've been going stir crazy waiting for it to happen. The monotony of my work days dragged out, spending every five minutes checking the local and national news for the headline I've been waiting for.

The police even came round. My heart almost flew out of my chest thinking I'd been caught before the media even got a sniff of it. I relaxed as soon as they mentioned it was just to have another look at Jim's room. I hadn't packed it up yet. I thought it would be suspicious for me to assume he wasn't coming back and get rid of his stuff.

Finally, day five though. It hit the papers. Apparently, according to the article headlined "JACK THE RIPPER IS BACK" a teenage boy was breaking into the factory to spray some choice words on the walls and came across my display. It says the police have a few leads and mentions this, that and the other about Sarah and her pursuits.

I will be keeping a copy of this. My first steps into notoriety. It has stirred some questions inside of me though. I need a way to be able to gain information about the killings from the perspective of the police. In order to ensure that no part of their investigations point towards me. That's one to mull over I think. I'm intelligent. Smarter than the detectives they probably have working on it. I can figure that out.

To the matter at hand now though, I need a new victim, a new location and a new display.

15/10/2006

What a stroke of absolute luck I have had this past week. I've let the dust settle on everything that has gone on. The investigation for the murder of Sarah/Sugar has hit a brick wall so I'm told and the search for Jim has turned up nothing, and there is no indication of his death.

Also, I have an inside track to the police force now, hence why I know about the prostitute investigation. On a random occurrence, in a bar, I happened across a not unattractive lady, who also works in the unit that handles that case. What a coincidence? I think not. I planned this. I knew who she was and where she worked. I followed her, found an excuse to meet her when she was out for a works party, and laid on the false charm. I can be quite charming when I want to be, and before the night was over, she was in bed with me.

Jenny Sullivan. A detective, but not on the case for Sarah, same department though, and that's good enough, and not too suspicious for me to ask if it pops up in the news. She's quite young for a detective, only a couple of years older than me. I will be having dinner with her tonight, and hopefully move this new relationship further forward.

I've had girlfriends before. It's all been part of my attempt to blend into normal society though. I've never had feelings for a woman, although I do enjoy the sex. It is a fraction of the satisfaction I get from when I kill though. Jenny was good in bed, aggressive. I like it when it's aggressive. I clamped my hands around her throat at one point and squeezed, lightly. The thought was in my head that I could take another kill right now, but I refrained, I need her, and it would launch a huge investigation if a detective went missing.

I have found my next victim too. A young man named George. From what I can tell he has just finished university, like me, and has made the leap to move to the big city. He is currently working in a call centre and lives alone. I believe he has only lived here a week and doesn't have many friends. I've only seen him with one other guy down a bar. He doesn't look tough, so I doubt he'll put up much of a fight, however, logistics still need to be worked out, and I must be prepared for anything.

Right now though, Jenny.

17/10/2006

I followed George after he finished work today, to a bar in the east of London. It's quite a distance from my flat, but the great thing about London is there is always a way home at the end of the night. I didn't want to take my car. My plan was to have a drink in the bar and find a way to introduce myself to George and his friend.

It went even better than I would have expected. His friend had to go early, leaving George to finish his drink on his own. He was sat at the bar, and I casually went up next to him and ordered a drink. It wasn't that busy so finding a spot directly next to him wasn't hard.

There was football on the television in the bar, and George seemed to be watching it, so I made a passing comment about it. I can't exactly remember what the comment was, but it caught his attention and started a conversation. As my drink came, I offered him one, and seeing as his friend had left him he seemed happy to have some company, and possibly make a new friend, I assume.

We talked for a couple of hours, about women and sport, all the while I was ordering shots, but disposing of mine while he wasn't paying attention. I feigned interest in what he had to say, but my mind was on the task. This was the night George was going to die, and I was going to be the one to help him on his way.

George lived near the bar, so when we left, I asked him which way he was going, and said that I lived a street across from him and knew of a shortcut.

The shortcut was down a dead end of a long alley, very secluded, only the back entrances to shops that were long shut by the time we got there. He didn't notice that it was a dead end till we got there, and he didn't notice the knife in my hand until it was sticking in his chest.

He was gone so quickly. I must have got the heart. He slumped towards me, but I took a step back and let him hit the floor avoiding getting blood on me. Time for my display. I was looking forward to this now more than the actual killing. Someone seeing the art that I had created out of something so gruesome.

George had a bag with him. In his bag was a laptop, a telephone headset, and some magazines about games. He actually reminded me of Jim briefly in that moment. I placed the serrated edge of my hunting knife in his mouth and began sawing. It was tough work, breaking his jaw and cutting until his head was almost separated. I pulled the top half of his head back, exposing the lower jaw and tongue. From his laptop, I removed keys from the keypad and placed them there, then took his telephone headset and placed them on his head, jabbing the plug end into his neck.

I took a step back to have a look at my masterpiece. It was beautiful. An ironic message about the scourge of the cold caller. That was what I was going for, but as before, the message doesn't really matter. It's all theatrics.

Scanning the area for any evidence I may have left, I once again took a last look at my work before leaving the scene. Careful to leave the alleyway without causing suspicion, I made it look like I went down there to take a piss. Before I knew it I was on a night bus home, free and clear. There was no link to me what so ever. It will be interesting to see how the press and police react to another killing in this manner.

18/10/2006

Not even a day has passed since George was added to my list and it has hit the headlines. "Serial Killer Terrorises London" was one headline, and a TV report has dubbed me "The Gallery Ripper". I'm assuming because of the way I have displayed my victims. I'm not a massive fan of this name, but in the scheme of things, it could be worse. I have been described as a "sadistic killer who likes to mutilate the bodies of victims to send a message about the modern society". I'm not sadistic, but I can see where they would get all that from. The media love to embellish. They will never just say, people are fucked up, and some people feel the need to kill. It's probably the displays, I bet secretly the press love the fact I do that, and hope one day they'll be able to snap a picture of them before the police get to take control of the crime scene.

Jenny is coming around this evening. Things have progressed nicely. I spoke to her on the phone earlier and she told me work is going mental, so she may be quite late. I can't wait to hear what she has to say about it all.

I am on the fence as to whether it would be too risky to attempt another kill straight away. The buzz around it is strong and I've got a feeling the streets of the city will be crawling with police. Maybe I shall wait a month. Patience is a virtue, and I should be conscious of the fact I do not intend to be caught. That's one thing they say about serial killers (yes, I have realised that is what I am and I wear the badge with a little bit of pride) is that they all secretly want to be caught. This is not true for me. I hands down do not want to be caught. I need to kill, something inside of me doesn't feel right if I don't. Getting caught would mean being put be in a jail cell for the rest of my life, probably in isolation. I'd never be able to kill again. I can't let that happen to me.

18/10/2006

Okay, so this is the first time I've written an entry twice in one day, but I am over the moon. Jenny is here, fast asleep, and she's told me some wonderful news. They have a lead on the murders. I should be panicking right? Wrong. The lead is not me. It's George's friend. Apparently he has a criminal record, and mysteriously disappeared last night. What an absolute stroke of luck. I just thought I should get it down while I have the chance. Jenny wants to spend the day together tomorrow. On a Friday! You'd think she'd have more work to do with what I've been getting up to. Never mind. She is my inside track. I shall keep her happy and take another sick day.

All told. With my extracurricular activities and my job, I am getting pretty tired and could do with a day off. Not sure what we will do though. Probably go out to the country or something. You always see couples doing that. I should get back to bed before she notices I'm not there.

31/10/2006

Halloween. What a perfect night for me to deconstruct a person. The great thing about Halloween is the blanket acceptance of people walking around dressed suspiciously, covered in blood and wearing a mask. A costume, a disguise won't go amiss whilst I stalk the streets of London.

I have my victim, I have my plan. It's genius, if I do say so myself. Jenny wants to go to a party that her work are holding. This is possibly the most genius part. I will be in a room surrounded by police. What a perfect alibi. I'll spend today telling Jenny that I am having stomach issues, and spend about half an hour at a time locked in the bathroom. This will allow me to do the same later at the party and be off the grid for at least thirty minutes without raising suspicion.

I have two costumes. Jenny wanted to go in a couple's costume, so I will first be going as Starsky, she will be Hutch. This is good, as people will see my face and also see me paired with Jenny, thus in their minds, definitively placing me at the party if for some reason an investigation begins to point towards me. The second costume, which I have already hidden in a secret location near the bar round the corner from the police station (This is where the party will be held) is the grim reaper. I couldn't resist. Plus it's covers me fully, allowing no recognisable features to be seen.

My victim works nights as a security guard at the grounds of a factory nearby. I will be able to get there, dispatch, display and be back at the party within twenty five minutes at a rush. I won't rush. I'll be careful, savour it.

The party starts at nine. It's six now, and Jenny is on her way over. I should really get ready.

01/11/2006

It's four in the morning. Jenny is asleep in my bed. The party was such a success, I am eager to see what happens when the world wakes up in a few short hours.

We arrived at the party fashionably late, around half past nine. Instantly people were greeting us and complimenting us on our costumes, especially Jenny, for her portrayal of an eighties icon. Lots of people were saying that they were glad they finally got to meet me and Jenny has been talking about me constantly. That is good, she must really like me. If I'm honest, I do have a slight bit of affection for her too, but that may because of the position she holds inside the police force and the use I have for her.

After a little while, possibly about an hour I made my excuses and headed towards the bathroom. To get to the toilets in that bar you had to walk into the little entrance way near the front door and go up some stairs. Instead of making the turn to go up the stairs, I exited the building, and before I knew it I was sprinting down the street towards the bag holding my hidden costume and instruments of death. My blood was really pumping with excitement.

I got to my bag, and hastily got changed out of sight. Once fully clothed and with my trusty old hunting knife in the back of my belt, I headed in the direction of the factory. The man I was looking for was quite large, but in an out of shape way, if things went wrong I would have no issues running away from him. His name was John. His friends called him big John. I suppose this is where he differs from the other two victims so far. He has friends, he has family. People who will miss him. These factors don't matter to me anymore. All that really matters is discretion and isolation of my victims. John's was perfect.

I got to the factory, and with a pair of snips, cut a hole in the fence, climbing through. The flowing gown of the grim reaper costume caught a little bit, it wasn't the most practical of costumes I have to admit, but it was the sentiment of the thing that really made me want to use it.

I knew John did a patrol every twenty minutes or so. He was pretty diligent about it too. Maybe he really took his job seriously, or maybe it was just an excuse to get out of his chair and have a wander around.

There was a path that ran around the outskirts of the factory. This is the route that John took first, before checking the fence line. I wanted to catch him here, before he would notice the hole I had created. I hid around one of the corners of the factory and waited for about five minutes before I heard his footsteps. I had timed this about right, in order not to be away from the party too long. I had already been gone ten minutes. I am hoping no one has gone into the toilet to check on me. Shit, I thought, why didn't I lock a cubicle and put some boots down to make it look like I was in there, Jenny will hopefully just tell people I'm fine and leave me to it. I cut these thoughts out of my head as John approached; there was nothing I could have done about it at that time.

I stepped out onto the path. John was about ten yards from me. I didn't say a word, just stood there silently with the knife behind my back. I imagine to John it looked like something out of a horror movie. He asked me who I was, and told me I shouldn't be there. I did nothing. He threatened me that he was going to call the police. Now I think of it, he should have kept to his threat, it may have saved his life. Eventually, after about a minute or two of this, he got frustrated, telling me to fuck off and taking a step forward.

I pulled the knife from behind my back. That slowed his advance. Not by much, but enough for him to proceed with a bit more caution. He told me to calm down and take it easy. I'd not even moved, I was calm; I was ready to take his life.

Without warning, taking me a bit by surprise, he lunged at me, grabbing the wrist of the arm which held my knife and knocked it out of my hand, pinning me up against the wall. Thank goodness I had been spending the last few months learning MMA. I unleashed several sharp elbows to the top of his head, then grabbed his wrist, twisting it with so much force it snapped. The crack was loud, his scream was louder as he collapsed to the floor clutching it. The noise was not part of my plan, I had to finish it quickly. I scrambled for my knife and with as much force as I could muster, slammed it into the side of his head, silencing him instantly.

I have to admit, this was not the way I wanted him to go, I wanted to enjoy it slightly more, not rush his death with a spur of the moment action. It doesn't really matter; I was on a strict timeline anyway.

I sat him up, and swiftly removed his eyes, placing them in his mouth, looking out. I also placed his baton that he failed to use in his hand and carved the words security into his chest, where a badge would usually go.

I took a step back and admired my work. Not my best out of the three, but it would do. I looked down at my watch and realised I had been gone for forty minutes. A quick scan of the area, another clean kill and I was off, through the hole, up the street and to my other costume. I quickly changed and before I knew it I was back in the bar, slightly sweaty from the running. Jenny did ask if I was okay, as I'd been gone a while, she asked if I wanted to go home. I said no. After that encounter with John, I was ready to party. I actually enjoyed myself in the wake of my deed. In a room full of police that had no idea who or what I was, and what was coming in the morning.

We got back to my place about an hour ago and made love. It was intensified every time I looked in her eyes and saw the affection she had for me. She had no idea the monster I was in the eyes of society. We finished, and cuddled for a bit, and slowly she drifted off to sleep. Before I started writing this, I checked the twenty four hour news. Nothing yet, but soon. A media storm was coming.

01/11/2006

I went to sleep after writing my last entry and was woken up at half six in the morning. Jenny had received a phone call asking her to go into work. It was happening. Her boss on the phone sounded panicked, and she was rushing around like a mad man looking for clothes to wear. It seems John had been found, and they were planning on increasing the manpower on the case. I tried so very hard to contain my smile, because I must have smirked at her. She asked me what I was finding so amusing. I was caught slightly off guard, but saved myself by saying maybe she wanted to think about running a brush through her hair before she leaves, as she was almost out the door with a ginger birds nest on her head.

She left, and I burst out of bed instantly and turned on the twenty four hour news. There it was. "The Gallery Ripper Strikes Again" scrolling across the screen. There was a reporter standing outside the factory, which was now filled with activity and surrounded by police tape.

She went on to describe the crime, in all its gory glory. She also went on to describe what a local psychologist thought about me. It was nothing special, nothing I hadn't already figured out on my own. He reached out and said I need help, and that he would be the one to offer it. I don't need help, I can't be helped, I don't want to be helped. I feel alive. I don't ever what to feel the indifference I felt as a teenager again. Everything is right for me.

As I was pondering on this thought, a news report flashed up. "Breaking News!!!". A female reporter, quite windswept, and clearly having been forced out of bed for this story, went on to suggest that the police have found important physical evidence which points towards a possible suspect.

I should be panicking. I should be packing a bag and my passport and heading to the nearest airport. But I'm not. Because I put that evidence there. The report doesn't tell you what it was, but I know it was a driving licence of a man I had met the week before. I casually took it from his wallet as he went to the bathroom. People tend to trust me, I can't imagine why.

I caught a brief glimpse of Jenny in the back ground doing something or other, I wasn't really thinking about her. I was thinking of ways I could tease the police into jumping to the wrong conclusions. The driving licence is just the tip of the ice berg.

01/12/2006

Christmas is rolling up fast. Jenny is happy, she says it's mainly because we are having our first Christmas together. It's only been two months and she has fallen for me. That's what I wanted. It's not without its downsides though.

She's always here. I'm finding it hard to get time to write this anymore, even when she is asleep, she will stir and wake up when I get out of the bed. I don't have time at work to do it, and I get home after her. I think she has unofficially moved in. I'm just waiting for her to broach the subject.

She keeps going on about the spare room as well. It isn't a spare room, it is Jim's room. I know he's never coming back, but I still haven't cleared up his stuff. I have sent a few things for his parents. Photos for them to distribute and trinkets that may hold some sort of sentimental value. They did ask, if I cleared the room, not to throw his stuff away, in case he returned. I just can't be bothered to clear it all out, it isn't at the top of my priorities at the moment.

Jenny is out looking for curtains with her friend, for my place. I'm just going to let it go. She has been very handy to have around, and I know the investigation has gone cold.

I've not done anything since John. Probably another reason why I haven't recorded anything in this diary, no exploits to put down. Although the urge is building, I want the trail to go completely cold before I tackle another victim. I can imagine this would drive the police insane. Jenny already seems frustrated when she tells me over dinner what is happening and how they are struggling to find this guy..."I'll give you a hint, he made you that carbonara" is what I was fighting not to say to her. I wonder how she would react if I did say that? Probably just laugh it off as a joke. I am known to be funny and tease with her. All part of my disguise as a human, when really I am a God. The God of death...that should have been my name, not the Gallery Ripper. Maybe I can change it? I'm not sure.

As the trail goes cold in the hunt for me, I feel it is almost time for the Gallery Ripper's next victim, something special this time...something to drive the media wild.

25/12/2006

Merry Christmas. My flat is full of people. My sister Gemma and her husband, my mother and Jenny's parents have come over for Christmas dinner. I have snuck out with my notebook for half an hour, saying I have to go drop off some presents to a friend. They didn't seem to mind. Having so many people round entertaining each other, they probably don't even notice I'm gone.

Our parents seem delighted that we are together. My sister made jokes to her husband James, and Jenny, that she had always worried about me, as I'd never had a girlfriend growing up. They all laughed, and even I smirked, I know now why I never did. I never needed one. Now I do, but not for the usual reasons. They all seem to be getting on famously, so it is nice for me to get away from it for a bit and be my actual self, if only on paper whilst sat down the road in my car.

The media is crazy again because of me. Jenny, luckily for her, avoided having to go into work though, which is good for her, bad for me. "A Christmas tragedy, designed by the Gallery Ripper" was the news this morning. My family have been talking about it most of the day. Speculating what sort of monster would do such a thing.

I decided to revisit the man whose driving license I had left with the security guard. His name was Geoff and he was a reasonably good man. He had a wife and two young boys. Last night, I went out for work drinks and he has a loose affiliation with the company I work for, and he was there.

I followed him home, at a distance, and as he drunkenly staggered to his door and unlocked it, I grabbed him, covering his mouth and dragged him into the passage down by the side of his house. I stabbed him repeatedly whilst still covering his mouth, until he was dead. I waited in the dark in silence for a while, making sure no one in the area or in his house had heard and been woken up.

I left his body there and entered the house. Perfect, pristine, with the Christmas tree glowing in the living room. There were several huge presents by the tree, I assumed they were for his kids. I took the boxes quietly outside, and expertly opened them, tipping the contents of the latest fad toys out onto the garden. Then I went to work. With a small hack saw I started to dismantle Geoff, loading him into the boxes, and finally re-wrapping them, and putting them back under the tree.

In the morning, so the news explained, his children got up early and began opening them without their parents there. They must have been horrified, scarred for life as they excitedly opened one of the boxes to see their daddy's head staring back up at them.

So far I believe this to be my masterpiece. I know it would be seen as cruel to damage the children like that and probably ruin every Christmas they ever will have, but I wasn't thinking about that. I was thinking about myself, my feelings, how it would look to them and how that would make me feel. It makes me feel amazing. Any morals I thought I may have had, have been washed away with this simple act. Nothing is taboo to me.

Jenny was saying that there is a good chance they will catch this man soon, as his killings are regular, and like most serial killers, he will eventually want himself to get caught. Not true. Even the fact he has killed someone he had previously used as a red herring is a sign that he is moving towards this. Again, not true. The reason I picked Geoff was simple, to get them scratching their heads, and think that they may be getting close. No doubt an interview will be heading my way, as with many people at the pub that night, but now I know most of the people involved in the investigation and they will recall me being at the party and with Jenny all night when I dispatched John.

She is right about one thing though. I should cool off for a bit. I've killed four people in less months. The more kills, the closer they'll get. I'll wait, hold back the urges, let it all settle for a while, then strike again in a monumental return to form.

10/06/2007

It's my twenty second birthday, and just fewer than six months since my last kill. I thought I'd give myself a birthday present. A macabre little gift, which fulfils everything I have been urging to do after the last entry.

Since my last entry, Jenny has moved in, and we are engaged. I've got a promotion at work, and she has been talking about how it would be the perfect time to start a family. I've never really thought about starting a family. Maybe having a protégé to carry on my work. I could mould that child into the perfect killer. I wonder what sort of complications having a family would present. I suspect it would not be easy to carry on. Even the looming marriage is making things difficult. It hasn't stopped me satisfying myself on my birthday though.

The victim: A homeless man called Alf, who wanders the streets at London with his dog, Shep. I know as a victim, it may be a step back for me. But I was seeing it as an experiment, plus, in the eyes of the law, a murder is a murder, and the return of the Gallery Ripper is as big a spectacle that the media could hope for.

Over the last few months, since the Christmas presents I left for Geoff's family, there have been odd mentions in the news. Asking "Where has he gone?" and "Will he ever be caught?" and finally, the question I just answered very early on the morning of my birthday "Will he ever strike again?". There has even been mention of Jim recently in the news, a follow up story with his family, pleading for anyone who may have seen him. It's not been linked to the Gallery Ripper case, and I have to say I'm surprised that nobody has stumbled across one of the bags I dumped across the countryside; I must have dug the holes deep enough.

Last night I went out for dinner with Jenny. We had an early, private celebratory meal on our own, before the party that will be held at the bar tonight, she's organising this now as I write. It was a nice dinner, no talk of her work, just focused on the wedding mainly. She got quite drunk actually, and fell asleep as soon as her head hit the pillow. I waited a bit, to make sure she didn't wake up again, even clapped loudly, nothing. Out the door I went, looking for Alf and Shep.

It didn't take me long to find them. They often move around in the same little area and find a spot to go to sleep that is under cover and hopefully warm for them. That spot all depends on if they get moved along or not by the police or security. I found them in the doorway of an Oxfam shop. I am guessing their thought is, a charity shop wouldn't deny a homeless man a little bit of shelter through the night, as long as they aren't there when the shop opens.

Shep woke up as I approached, followed quickly by Alf. I've spoken to them a couple of times over the last couple of months. A lot more recently, as I was gearing up to my present to myself. They were pleasant enough to me, and Alf smiled as he saw me. I handed him a warm drink I had brought with me and a small piece of ham for Shep. I know what I was about to do would be classed as disgraceful, but Alf really didn't have anything to live for, apart from Shep, and Shep could be adopted after Alf was gone. Not that I really care about any of that, I just thought I should at least give a man who has nothing a little bit of kindness, before I ended his misery. Does this make me a good person? I very much doubt it.

I sat with them for a bit, and Alf told the story of how he got Shep. The more he went into it, the more bored I became of him. How selfish must a man be to deny a pet he claims to love a warm home and a loving family. I even think they do it sometimes to earn themselves more money, through sympathy for the dog. People are suckers for a pet. Not me. Before he got to the end of his story, I plunged the knife into his chest. I was a bit rusty, so I adjusted and thrust again, piercing his heart. He died quickly with a look of shock in his eyes. Shep looked at me and Alf's body inquisitively.

He didn't bark or growl. He just laid his head on Alf's lap and let out a whimper.

I moved the body out of the shop doorway. I did make sure there were no cameras or people about. London can be busy, even at stupid o'clock in the morning. There was no one. I moved him down the street slightly and sat him up, covering his chest wounds with his coat. I laid out a sign saying "Please give generously", and attached Shep's lead to Alf's arm. Then I walked away.

No major display this time, no gore for people to be shocked at. This is my experiment, how many people will walk by unaware of the dead man they are passing? How many people will even put money in a hat I have put out for him? How long, before someone cares enough to check if this vagrant is okay. I can now enjoy my birthday knowing he's out there, quietly collecting coins in his hat, never to spend them.

13/06/2007

Three days! He sat there with Shep for three days. God knows how the dog survived. I would think people thought Alf was asleep and gave him bits of food as they passed.

I walked past on the second day to see if he was still there. He was in the same position. Unmoved. I checked his hat. He had about five pounds in it. People were generous, but no one actually cared.

The killing hasn't officially been linked to my previous works; the display was a tad subtle for that. But Jenny has hinted that the weapon used matches the wounds on victims from a previous case. A piece of information they haven't released to the press. Probably smart, I think the press would have a field day. Maybe I should tip them off. Perhaps I will.

16/06/2007

In the style of Jack the Ripper, I have written a letter to the news, and it has hit the headlines in a big way. It went as follows:

'To whom it may concern,

I am the Gallery Ripper, and I have killed again. The homeless man and his dog was me, my display, my gift to you all. I have no intention of stopping and have plans for future masterpieces to be released to the world. I cannot be stopped, I cannot be caught.

I will kill indiscriminately until the end of my days.

Regards,

'The Gallery Ripper'

I admit it is a bit dramatic, but I wanted to take credit for my work. That appears to have become a big part of the satisfaction I get from it now. I wrote the letter on a computer to avoid hand writing recognition, and I drove thirty miles to post it. No doubt that area will be a source for the police to search for me.

The letter was printed repeatedly in many of the major newspapers; however the police so far are denying that the it is genuine. I suppose there is no way to check if it is, without me telling them in person. I would be intrigued to see what the police officers I have come to know quite well through Jenny would think if I walked into the station covered in blood telling the truth of who I was.

08/07/2007

My wedding day is in two weeks. Jenny is doing a lot of the preparations for it, I have little input, as long as I turn up she will be happy. That suits me just fine. I want to get another kill in before hand, to relax me and quell the urges before the honeymoon, you never know, I may even enjoy the holiday after a kill.

I've picked out my victim. It is an actress named Katie. She's not famous, but she has done a couple of stints on the television and a few small parts in films. It's something a bit more high profile. The media will love it. They must secretly love me. I must have sold so many papers for them over the last year.

Katie is quite talented. After her death she will probably be hailed as a great actress that could have one day been a Hollywood star, but had her flame blown out far too early. The chances are that wouldn't be true, but embellishment sells stories, and I'm not going to argue with that.

I'm sure people would say that I am doing this because I want to be famous. I can see why people would think that, but it's not really true. In order to be famous, I'd have to be caught. I would like my work to be notorious though. I'd like to be unknown forever, much like Jack the Ripper. When I set out killing, this was not my goal. My goal was to feel, something. Anything. I find the further I go with it, the more of a rush I get. I can't go backwards, it feels like an addiction. An addiction I don't want to stop.

Katie is doing a play in a small theatre over towards Dalston in a week's time. I have my ticket. I will sit in the audience quietly watching, knowing that will be the last time anyone will see her alive on the stage. After the play, I will wait at the stage exit for her, probably with other fans waiting to say hello. I'll be patient, I'll take my time. Eventually she will be alone, no one will be around, and that's when I will strike.

I haven't figured out how I will display her. On previous occasions I have just decided at the time, apart from Alf. That one was planned for my own interest. I think preparation and planning is key for my displays now though. In order to avoid detection and increase the shock and awe that can be gained from them. This one will have to be theatrical.

16/07/2007

It all went better than planned. Katie is dead. I killed her. I waited by the stage exit, but she never came out. All the other actors did, followed by the stage hands, the director and everyone else that worked on the production. I overheard the director telling one of the fans that she often stayed behind to have the stage to herself, and locks up after. A strange occurrence for a theatre to let an actress do that, maybe she knew the owner or something? At least she was dedicated to her art form. Just as I'm dedicated to mine.

This was perfect for me. I waited another half an hour, and then entered through the stage door. It was a small theatre, no security to speak of. I dead bolted the door behind me as I entered and checked the other doors were locked. The theatre was dark. In the background, from the stage I could hear her singing.

A young girl, alone, in this area, I'm surprised no one saw this coming? No one offered to stay behind and keep her company. I stood in the wings, watching as she belted out a ballad without the addition of music. She really was talented; I almost didn't want to strip the world of that talent. But I'd come this far, the blood was pumping; there was no way I was going to walk away from this.

I stalked my way onto the stage. She was so engrossed in her performance; she didn't even hear me when the boards creaked. As she lifted her head to hit one of the more prominent notes in the song, I ran my knife across her throat. This was her best performance. She didn't fall to the ground straight away. She turned and looked at me in the eye. Confusion and fear had swept over her, and then she fell. A true performer.

I used the stage equipment for my display. I cut her throat open to reveal her vocal chords and set a scene. The stage was already prepared for one of the opening scenes of the play ready for the next day. I found her costume, dressed her and positioned her where she would be when the curtains went up. I went to the stalls and took a seat, remembering the performance she gave earlier that night. It was perfect. Once satisfied, I slipped out one of the fire exits, leaving the theatre sealed from the inside.

I got home quite late. Jenny was waiting for me, wedding magazines and brochures open all over the table. She was worried that the wedding wasn't going to be perfect. I reassured her and packed the things away. She asked where I had been, I just told her I had work to finish off before I could leave the office, this often was true, so it was believable. I kissed her goodnight and let her drift off to sleep. Watching her, I did think about how we'd spend our lives together. Being closest to me, would she ever find out my real secrets? Would she be able to accept me for who I really was. I doubted it, she was dedicated to her work, there was no way she wouldn't take me in if she found out.

30/07/2007

I'm a married man. I never would have thought it would have happened. Jenny is so happy. Both our families are happy for us. I'm even content with the situation. We took our honeymoon in Mexico. It was sunny and relaxing. I barely thought about killing when I was out there. Seeing off Katie did the trick. I often thought about how the police investigation was going. No doubt they would be interviewing everyone who was at the play the night before. It doesn't worry me too much, I bought my ticket in cash and used a false name for everything. I thought about bringing it up with Jenny, but I decided against that, I didn't want to arouse suspicion. We arrived back, and there weren't police waiting to cart me away, I took that as a sign that I was in the clear. At least for now.

We got home and unpacked everything. The flat was a mess from all the wedding presents. Blenders and toasters everywhere. We settled, switched on the TV and relaxed. Jenny disappeared to the bathroom, and I flicked through the channels. I was exhausted. It's amazing how relaxing can take it out of you.

She was in the bathroom for quite a while. I had settled on a true crime documentary about a serial killer. I felt smug as they went on about the pitfalls this man had found to get caught. I took mental notes of things to avoid and thought about my next kill. I would have to wait a bit I think. It would probably be suspicious if the killings started again as soon as we got back from the honeymoon. A couple of months should be sufficient.

Jenny came back in, and sat down next to me. I didn't take too much notice as I was engrossed in my show. She was beaming a smile. Eventually she nudged me. I looked over at her, and I think at that point I knew what was coming. She waited for a moment. A moment too long, I had to ask "What?" She continued smiling at me, and a moment later she said the words I was waiting for. "I'm pregnant". My world was ripped apart. I faked happiness. But how was I going to kill with a baby? When Jenny is not around, I'll have to look after it, and the rest of the time Jenny will be there. I can't just sneak away, do a bit of murder and sneak back. What if she wakes up in the middle of the night to the baby crying and I'm not there? As it stands, I don't know what I am going to do. I could run away? I could just drop everything and get on a plane, and disappear, start somewhere fresh. Become the ripper in another city. I will have to think about it.

04/01/2008

We are six months into the pregnancy. I've not killed anyone since Katie. Every day is a struggle not to grab, strangle, stab, display someone. It really is a struggle. No one can understand this. Well, maybe other people in my position, but they don't exactly advertise themselves for a support group.

I check the news everyday for someone taking on my mantle. A copycat, some mention of the Gallery Ripper. Nothing. It's frustrating. I should be out there. I should be doing it. It was all going so well, but now I resent this child already for snatching my happiness away from me.

Jenny is frustrated and uncomfortable. Without the outlet I need to find relaxation and happiness I find myself resenting her as well. I know it's not her fault. This was my plan, my design. All this was fabricated to fulfil my own needs, and now it has blown up in my face. I really don't know what to do. Like a heroin addict, I will just have to take the pain I'm feeling. For now anyway. I can't foresee a future where I don't kill. I'll have to find a way.

The child is a girl. We wanted to know. Jenny couldn't wait to find out, and she is over the moon. She wanted a little princess. When I thought briefly about having a child, a prodigy to carry on my work. To teach how to kill and get away with it, I never imagined it being a girl. I'm not sure I can imagine ever being able to bond with this child.

We have been decorating the baby's room. Jim's stuff is gone. Jim is forever lost; nobody has stumbled across him and the search as long but dwindled. I occasionally think back about Jim, with fondness I add. He was the catalyst, the thing that spurred me on to be the man I am today. If I'm honest and think about it properly, the way I am today stems all the way back to the psychologist who urged me to write this diary and explore my feelings. I can't say if I hadn't started this I would have ever taken the leap to killing people. Hell, it was even Jim finding this diary that got me to kill him!

I read somewhere, possibly on the internet, that one in a hundred people are classed as psychopaths. If this were true, why do none take the step that I have taken? Is it because more than that there is something fundamentally wrong with me? Or was it just that the circumstances were perfect for me? Like a perfect storm? It doesn't feel wrong for me. It feels empowering. Like I'm the apex predator.

One thing this child, and hiatus from killing has done, is cause me to be more reflective on my life and the things that have led me to this point. I smile when I think about everything I have achieved, like an actor looking back on their body of work. I'm proud of what I've done. I'll have to bide my time, but I know one thing for certain. It's not over yet.

10/04/2008

My child has arrived. Slightly early, but not massively. Leah Suzanne
Mason.

It was eleven in the evening, and I was at a bar with a couple of
acquaintances from work. One of them had just got a promotion and
insisted on a few of us going to celebrate with him. So there we all were, I
was jovial on the surface. I'd been playing the happy soon to be father
role quite well the last three months. Inside I was dying, dreading what
was to come.

I got the phone call from Jenny's mother and took it outside. She had
gone into labour and was on her way to the hospital. I instantly ran back
inside to tell the others why I had to leave early. They all cheered me on
my way. Hopefully the dread in my heart wasn't too obvious on my face.

I began walking at some pace, realising that I was also quite tipsy from the
drink. I was taking shortcuts to the tube, down dark alleys that I knew
would take minutes off my journey. I'd been down them during the day,
and I knew they were rough areas not to be taken at night, but I wasn't
worried, I knew I could handle myself if I needed too.

I did need to.

Two young gang members were waiting at the end of one of the alleys for
me. I'd taken a wrong turn, and this one was a dead end. I had got to
them by the time I realized this. They were on me instantly as I tried to
turn around, one had a knife in his hand. If only I had my hunting knife
with me, I would have been as smug as Crocodile Dundee. "That's not a
knife" I would have said with a fake Australian accent and a smirk. But I
didn't have it with me, why would I, I haven't taken it out of its hidden
space for over six months. I tried to talk my way out of it, my mind was on

getting to the hospital to meet the most destructive thing in my life, my daughter.

They were having none of it. This was their mistake. They should have let me go. With lightning fast reactions, sobering up instantly, I grabbed the one with the knife by the wrist, turning it with a crack and inserting the knife into his stomach. He fell to the ground as I span and punched the other one, also knocking him down. I pulled the knife from the first one's stomach, he yelped, but I ignored it as I thrust it back into his chest three more times. Then I turned my attention to the second man, trying to get to his feet. The knife was in my hand, blood dripping down the blade. He looked at his friend and lost his nerve. He sprinted for the end of the alley.

I didn't chase him. There was no way he was going to contact the police, at least not straight away. I turned my attention back to the body of the man I had just killed. I pulled out his wallet and looked at his ID. His name was Kevin. How odd I'd thought that he had my name, yet he was nothing like me at all. Before I knew it, I was scalping him. My hands moving like I'd done it only yesterday. I had no plans to create a display tonight, yet I was. I was me again. I took the money from his wallet and tucked it in under his scalp, then one by one cut off his fingers, placing them in each of his pockets. A brief reference to stealing I thought.

I looked at my watch, I didn't have time to admire my work, I had to get myself cleaned up and get to the hospital. My flat wasn't too far away after the tube, so I ran there and changed, washing the blood off my hands and throwing my clothes in the wash. I looked almost respectable again as I set off towards the hospital.

When I got there, the birth was over. It was quick. Jenny's mother scolded me for being late, and told me my sister and mother were on their way. They'd be a couple of hours yet. They were more enthusiastic than me, they could have just waited till the morning. But that isn't like them I suppose.

I walked into the delivery room. Jenny was asleep. Then I saw her, next to Jenny's bed in a small cot on wheels. The most beautiful creature I have ever seen. She was gorgeous. I leant over the cot and couldn't stop staring at her. I've never felt love for another person before. Not properly, not Jenny or my family. But her, little Leah, she was mine. She was my world now. I didn't even think about the killing in that moment, or if Leah would be able to be a part of that. I didn't care. All I cared was that she was here, and she was mine. The killing would have to stop. All my attention would be on this angel. Maybe one day, she will turn out to be like me, and I can teach her, but that was just a brief thought at the back of my mind. I love her, and nothing in this world will take her away from me, of that I can be certain.

17/04/2008

My daughter is a week old. The love I felt at the hospital has not faded over the time. It wasn't just adrenaline from the kill earlier in the night as I suspected later on that evening. It is pure, unhinged crazy love for another human being. She is part of me. It has affected me massively. I've not been scouring the papers or the news for words on my offing of the mugger. He has featured and it has been linked to the other Gallery killings. I'll give the police one thing. They are good when it comes to reconstructing crimes. They found it glaringly obvious that I was attacked and defended myself, and the display was an afterthought. They even recognised that there could have been a second man there, and put out a request for him to come forward, with no repercussions if he did.

Three days ago he did come forward. He even gave an interview on the news. I was worried for a moment as he would have seen my face and been able to give an accurate description of me, but from what it seems, and what Jenny has heard from her colleagues in passing, he was no use whatsoever, it was dark and he said it all happened so fast. He left out the part that he was trying to mug me, surprisingly, and he is now being hailed as the man who met and survived the Ripper.

I wasn't worried for myself when he appeared on the screen. I was worried for Leah. I didn't want to be taken away from her so soon after getting her. I didn't want her growing up being told her father was a monster. I wanted to guide her, lead her towards the path that I had found, so she could experience the joy I have. The power I have. The feeling of being a God, in charge of life and death. I don't think it's wrong for me to want my child to experience the height of happiness. Don't all parents want that? The difference is, I know how to achieve it.

She's not going to be old enough for a while. I think in the wake of all that has happened, and a witness coming forward, it's probably best for me to put my needs to one side and store these feelings away somewhere safe until I believe she is ready.

12/01/2009

Jim has finally been found. I can't believe it, after all this time. I suppose with weather and such it was inevitable that he would be found eventually, well pieces of him anyway.

I sit watching the news with Leah on my lap. It's been nine months since she was born, and nine months since I've killed. It seems some kids were building a fort in one of the areas where I had buried part of him. They were digging and came across one of the bin bags. They've only found the one, but police are now putting a search out across the county. I assume it won't be too long before they find some other parts of him.

His parents are understandably devastated, and the police have been over to tell me the news. Jenny was sympathetic, and I said I'll have to try to be strong for his parents. He was my best friend after all. I said I wasn't too shocked, after all this time it was pretty obvious he wasn't going to turn up alive, but it's always good to keep hoping.

It's not been linked to my other murders. It's nothing like them, no display, no pride in it. I couldn't have done that with Jim, it was too close to home, too many fingers would point in my direction. I'm worried they will now.

I took a slight bit of pride in my work as I watched the news and whispered in Leah's ear "Daddy did that". She's too young to understand, but it's a nice feeling to be able to take credit to another person, briefly revealing myself to someone who won't judge me.

The police asked me some probing questions about Jim, nothing they hadn't asked me already, and I remembered the answers I had given previously, so there was no suspicion. I don't think they are even thinking it could be me, a few of the officers knew Jenny, and me, and would never have thought I was capable of such a thing. To them I am a meek, loving and caring man. I wanted it that way, and with Leah and Jenny by my side, it was almost true.

The funeral is going to be soon, I will attend. I don't particularly want to, but I will. I should thank Jim for everything I have now. He'll probably be cursing me from the afterlife, but what he should know, is in being my first, and setting me on this path, he truly was my best friend. Ha, if people only knew how I treated my best friend, I wouldn't have any at all.

As I write this, I think about how things happened with Jim. I go over it in my head making sure I did do everything to ensure it could not be traced back to me. I know it can't. But the worry is still there, it stems from Leah I think. This child has changed me so much. I never would have fathomed it two years ago. How different I was back then.

13/01/2009

Jenny is dead. I am sitting on a plane currently heading to Africa. Kenya to be exact. Leah is with me. I had planned for this over the years. But the way it has come about was purely my own fault.

I had left my notebook containing these writings out. I had just finished my last entry, and was distracted by Leah, not that I'm blaming her, I should have known better. I was always so careful with this book, finishing my entries alone, no distractions or onlookers, then placing it under a floorboard in the bedroom I had loosened when Jenny started spending more time here. I covered it with a rug, and had a decorative trunk placed on top of that. Nobody would have had a clue that this existed without actively searching for it.

Part of me thinks that subconsciously I may have left it out on purpose, I've always gone against the idea that all killers want to be caught, I guess maybe I wanted to be recognised, not caught. I wouldn't be on this plane if I wanted to be caught. I am so infatuated with Leah, feelings that I never really felt for Jenny, maybe in some small corner of my mind I wanted to cut Jenny out of our lives and have my daughter all to myself?

It's too late to try and figure this out though. I had left my notebook on the side table as I was completing my last entry. Leah was crying and wanted to be changed. Jenny had been out with her friends. She was making the most of the fact I didn't mind being left with the baby, having time to myself.

I didn't hear her come in. She was a bit tipsy, but not drunk and had sat herself down in the chair where I was writing my thoughts, to take off her shoes. She must have noticed the book, having never seen it before, and I'm guessing the detective in her couldn't resist having a peek. When I came into the living room she was reading it, tears flooding down her face. She must have been caught up in what I had written, because she didn't hear me grab a kitchen knife or sneak up behind her. Why she didn't phone the police as soon as she knew what she was reading I have no idea. Maybe she couldn't bring herself to believe it. Without thought or hesitation, I ran the knife across her throat and stabbed her in the chest twice. I could hear Leah crying in the other room, but she would have to wait. I wonder if I will tell her what I did to her mother? Whether she would care or not? That's a problem for the future.

There was no time for a display for Jenny; I left her on the floor, one shoe off. I needed to get Leah and get moving. I have over the years been sending money to a hidden foreign bank account for this very scenario, it was up to about ten thousand pounds, enough to get somewhere and start fresh. The account was untraceable, and Jenny didn't really pay much attention to my money, we still kept separate bank accounts.

I packed a few things, clothes and this notebook, then scooped Leah into my car and headed straight for the airport. I figure I would have about twenty four hours before Jenny would be discovered, that was enough time for me to disappear with my daughter. One of the first things I did was ensure that Leah was able to travel on my passport.

We got to the airport and I booked a ticket to the first flight with open seats. Kenya. It didn't matter that I put this on my credit card; I wouldn't be staying there long. The key was to stay below the radar and keep moving. I had managed to obtain a fake passport through someone I met online a while back. I would use this to cross the African borders and keep moving.

The airport was surprisingly easy to get through. We were questioned as to why I was travelling last minute with my daughter, it was just an off the cuff comment by one of the customs officers, but to avoid arousing suspicion I told them my mother lived in Africa and had fallen ill. They seemed happy with that, and even wished her well as we left.

Now I'm on the plane, enjoying a whisky and watching my daughter sleep. She had a few problems when we took off with her ears popping, she did not like that at all. I have noticed over the past few months, she will make noise and scream, but I've never seen her cry. Maybe she is going to be more like me than her mother. That is a good thought.

I am thinking about Jenny. I spent so long with the woman that it's hard not to. I never loved her, but she was part of my life. I wonder how the investigation will go once she is discovered. Once they found out I have fled the country. Will they attribute it to the Gallery Ripper?

My knife! I have left my hunting knife in the flat. A thorough search would have them find it under my secret floor board. They will know who I am. No doubt there will be a man hunt. I don't know how I feel about this. I have done everything required not to be caught though. I am confident we will be fine. I'll be Leah's world, and she will be mine. Father and daughter on the run together.

10/06/2013

It has been nearly three years since I murdered my wife and went on the run with my daughter. We have travelled the world and flown below the radar, avoiding detection at every turn.

I did follow the news for a bit following our departure from the UK, and was surprised to see that Jenny's death, although attributed to me, was not actually linked to the Gallery Ripper cases. This is the reason for this entry. I am sat on the beach, I won't say where, with my five year old daughter Leah playing in the waves.

Enough time has passed for me to reveal the identity of the Gallery Ripper to the world. After this entry I shall place this notebook in an envelope and post it to the head office of the metropolitan police. That will give away my location, so following posting it, we shall move on.

Since we fled the UK, we have crossed several borders and worked our way from country to country without being caught. I have killed several times along the way, however I have refrained from leaving a display for the world, that would be far too easy to track my movements if I had.

Leah is blossoming. She has become the perfect lure, leading unaware victims to me ready to be dispatched.

I'm not sure if she is fully aware of what is going on, or thinks it's a game, but it has become the norm for her and one day, I'm sure, she will kill too. I saw her playing with the corpse of a stray dog recently before a bystander moved her away, in that moment, I actually felt proud.

So, here it is. For the police in all its glory. It is not a manifesto, but my story. I am Kevin Mason, and I am the Gallery Ripper. I have killed many people, and have never been caught. I will kill many more, and will never be caught.

 For the final time,

Hasta luego.

Following the arrival of the package from Thailand, Kevin Mason has not been seen or heard from since. Neither has Leah Mason.

Steven Griffiths would like to thank everybody involved in the development of this novella. Most of all, Casey Allum, a talented portrait artist, for all her hard work on the cover design.

About the Author

Steven is a former aircraft technician in the British Army, and a recent graduate from the University of Cumbria. He currently lives in London and has written several screenplays along with this novella He is now working on his next novel.... For anyone who is worried, no, he is not a serial killer.

Look forward to the next instalment from Steven Griffiths featuring Kevin Mason in "Hunting a Psychopath".

14478600R00048

Printed in Poland
by Amazon Fulfillment
Poland Sp. z o.o., Wrocław